Dedication

This is to all the young kids with dreams and my loving family, Manley James Sr., Charlene James, Manley James Jr., and Blake James.

Chapter 1

"Wake up honey" said my mom. I'm a typical 14 year old except I feel like I have the best boyfriend in the world his name is Christopher but I call him Chris. By the way, my name is Taylor this book I guess will be fun or sad I'm not sure I will write when something happens. I got out of my bed and turn my bath tub water on. When I got in the bath tub I saw scales " aww a tale what is this".

Out of nowhere a lady with a tale popped up and told me everything she said "you are now a mermaid accept this I'm your life and you may not tell anyone this". I thought mermaids were a myth I felt like I was about to throw up but I also felt excited.

If only I knew what to do. I got out and I tried touching the person to see if she was real but she moved back every time I reached out. She told me her name was Layla and that I have powers now and I will see them after a while. I still couldn't believe this, it can't be true at all. I wiped off my body and then the tail went away, when I looked up Layla was gone.

I went to go get my phone to see if my boyfriend texted me but not one text. This is so unusual because he texts me every day. I don't even understand this day it is way too much and it's just this morning. I don't even know if you guys want to read this ever since I started writing this bad things happened. How is my life going to be now?

Can I tell my boyfriend this or my mom or dad? OMG THIS HAS TO BE A DREAM.

I slapped myself while my eyes were closed then I went in the bathroom and poured water on myself next I waited and no tale. But then, I suddenly fell to the ground and I had a tale. Why is this happening to me what have I done ever? Maybe this was meant to be maybe I'm like the chosen one or whatever those people do and say. "Taylor hurry up your going to miss the bus" I quickly got dressed and ran downstairs, then I ran outside to catch the bus.

I kind of sit alone the bus but talk to my friends in front or behind me there awesome but, I can't tell them what just happened. I sat down in my seat and text Chris. "oh Tay Tay on the bus" said my friend Lisa she's cool but, she is way way too loud for me. I said "hey" to all my friends and just got in my seat to wait for Chris to reply. Finally, I heard my phone Bing and I looked at it and Chris replied saying "sorry about that I had a rough morning and I missed the bus so ttyl and see you soon love you" I replied but not saying what I texted back. "Get off the bus you crazy kids" said my bus driver I don't know his name but, all I know is that it starts with an A because everyone says "bye A something" but I can never tell. "Aww" I said as I rolled down the bus stairs. Chris was right there in front of me he helped me. "Surprise I thought you would like my little lie" said Chris.

"Thanks for coming" I said as he helped me up, "I just wish you have surprised me when I was off the bus because that hurt a lot and I mean a lot". He kissed me on my forehead and walked me to class. My teachers name is Mrs. Kayaks but, she wants us to call her Mrs. K so I do. I walked to my desk and blew a kiss to Chris and mouthed "bye".

When I sat down my friend came up to me and asked me if I knew the secret, I replied by saying "what secret wait hold up I'm not supposed to tell anyone" and then she said "wait ok slow your roll I'm talking about Kristin and Marcus because their going out now what are you talking about" I didn't know what to say.

Do I run away or act like I do there her or what? Now I am really scared, she is just waiting there for a reply geesh what have I done now. "Ok if you're not going to tell me then I am just waiting my time so bye" said Jayla aka my friend the one talking about the secret. This is my first time being in a situation like this. First the mermaid thing, next my boyfriend scaring me, and now my friend knowing I have a secret. What else can go wrong today? Wait hold up you guys reading this can't tell anyone or show this book to anyone or it will let my secret out to anyone.

"Okay class please sit down and take out your binders" said Ms. K. I was pulling out my binder but then, my staple on my notebook cut me. Trust it really really hurts like crazy. "Ok everyone should have their stuff out now I will pair you with a partner and work on everything you know about Egypt" said Mrs.K.

When she called my name I heard her say with Justin. The background story about him and I is that he likes me and my boyfriend and him hate each other. Last year, when I was 12 Justin kissed me on the lips and Chris saw him then, punched him. They got in a fight but no one knew about it except for Chris, Justin, and me. I went to Justin and sat at his desk. It actually wasn't that bad he just wanted to work nothing more. After we were done, Mrs.K asked us what we knew. Justin and I only got 12 ideas but, we read them anyway. When it was time for lunch, Chris met me at the door entering the cafeteria. I felt like someone was staring and me and I turned around. When I turned around it was Justin.

Chapter 2

When I turned around it was Justin staring at me but, he turned away really quick. I kind of feel bad for him because he is a really nice guy but, I'm taking and he is not really my type. Chris and I found a seat in the cafeteria and sat there alone. We always just talk about how much we love each other and what are wedding will look like. Chris is everything I dreamed of I mean everything. He is there for me when I need him, smart, hot, and loves me. If only people knew the love we had for each other. So, I skipped threw the whole day but, finally I am home. I went in the kitchen and saw a note that my mom and dad won't get back home until tomorrow. I went upstairs and called Chris. I invited him over. When he got there we watched a movie, and ate popcorn. When I was getting the water it spilled all over me. I ran upstairs really fast. I went in my bathroom shut the door and locked it.

I look around for a towel but, I fell because the tail came back. Chris came running upstairs he knocked on the door and asked "is everything ok do you want me to come inside" I replied by saying "no" quickly. I started wiping my body off with the towel and my tail went away. I got up and came out the door. Chris walked me downstairs and asked "what happened". I just told him that I didn't want you to see me like that. After everything, we finished watching the movie and finished eating our popcorn. He got all his stuff and left after the movie. I went upstairs and looked up how to get rid of a mermaid tail. But then, Layla appeared.

She turned off my laptop and said "are you crazy, you can't look up things like that and you need to be a lot more careful, your identity is about to be given away". I didn't know what to say I just froze she appeared out of nowhere and scared the mess out of me. Who does she think she is, just appearing in my house like that? "Why are you here and stop scaring me" I said. "First off you need to shut up because I'm trying to help you" replied Layla. She just told me to shut up. We started arguing but then she said "I'm not trying to harm you, Chris and your family are so close to find out that you're a mermaid. If they find out much more than relief will happen, you could not walk again or people could think you're crazy". I looked at her like she was crazy. "So you're trying to tell me that if my love ones find out this secret something dark could happen. Answer this, could they get hurt"? I said. "Yes they could get hurt or could never remember you ever. In mermaid world, if a secret is revealed the love one will lose their memory and never remember you or your secret" replied Layla. I got off my bed and put my hands on my head. I fell to the ground and started crying. Layla sat down beside me and told me her story. She lost everyone because she loved them enough to not let anything happen to them. I never ever thought of it like that but, now I know not to tell anyone. I went in the bathroom and wiped my face off. I called Chris and talked to him all night. When I woke up I noticed I was on my bedroom floor with my phone on top of me. I noticed that I talked to Chris until I fell asleep. I got off the floor and got dressed, washed, and ate breakfast. When I was walking out the door my mom and dad were coming in.

They kissed me on my forehead and said "you are so mature and I am proud of you". I saw the bus so I went running. When I got on the bus, my friend McKenna sat in the seat with me. She told me that she knows my secret. I asked her "what secret I don't have a secret". She kinda freaked me out because I thought she was talking about me being a mermaid. I got up and started screaming "YOU KNOW NOTHING ABOUT ME SO JUST LEAVE ME ALONE". She replied by saying "you need to calm down, I was just saying I knew you and Justin have a thing". What was she talking about I completely like Chris. She is totally out of her mind today I have never met anyone crazy like her before.

Chapter 3

"What are you talking about" I asked. She never had the chance to reply because we were already at school. I got off the bus and met Chris at the front door of the school. We walked together to my class and kissed good bye like usual. When I got in my class, I took out my iPad and looked at my grades. I noticed that I had all A's. I was so happy because I thought I was failing after all that has happened. I went in the back of the room to go to Justin. I asked him if he told anyone we had a thing for each other. "No why would you say that you know I HATE YOU" said Justin.

What why would he hate me I thought him and I were friends. This can't be true. "I thought we were friends" I said. "Are you crazy? You let your boyfriend beat me up and didn't talk to me until yesterday so, if you thought we were friends I feel sorry for you"! Said Justin. I walked away but, I felt really sad. I never thought of it like that,

I feel so stupid, mean, and dumb. I can't believe I ruined our friendship. I turned around but, he just rolled his eyes and turned away. I sat down in my seat and texted Chris that I feel really sad. When it was time for lunch Chris and I sat down. We talked about why I was sad. He felt so sorry for me and cuddled with me at the table. After the day was over, I sat on my bed and I started to cry.

I never thought I was that mean. When I was 7, Justin and I were like best friends. Everything changed in middle school. "Taylor come down dinner is ready" said my mom. I ran downstairs and sat at the dinner table. "Sweetie what took so long, you look like something's bothering you"? Asked mom.

"Mom no, I know that you love me and want to make sure I am alright but, something's are just are not meant to be said" I replied. "Ladies ladies let's just have a nice dinner and talk about my day" said dad. Dinner was so good today, I had spaghetti, Italian bread, and corn. It was delicious I mean for real. I got up from the table quick because someone was at the door. I ran to the door and opened. "Hey I have something important for you but first are you Taylor" said the guy at the door. "Yes of course but why" I replied. He handed me a package and ran off. I ran upstairs and put it on my bed then went back downstairs to finish eating. When I was done I went in my room and opened the package with my door locked. It was a book about Mermaid identity with a sticky note on it that said hide this somewhere safe and secure. Since I think I heard someone coming I hid the book behind my pillow and acted like I was doing homework. When I heard that person go away I took the book out and started reading it. It has 768 pages. It told me all about Mermaid world and keeping your identity safe. I put the book in a secret place and took a nap. During my nap I had a dream that I told my family and boyfriend and I lost my legs and whenever I saw them they never remembered me so, it was a nightmare.

My boyfriend didn't even recognize me it was really hard for my life because nobody even knew I existed. Anyway, I got out of bed and went to my bathroom. I washed my face and started to think. If I don't tell them and they find out they will hate me and I have more drama but, if I do tell them they won't hate me and my relief is gone but I will lose my legs so that's the bad thing. I went to my mom to go talk to her. "Mom how do you tell someone something so deep and you might lose them" I asked. "Is it boy drama or what and sweets you should always do what is right" my mom explained. She went back downstairs. Like that helped a lot I could have called dad. I hate my life now or I love it and I'm just in a midlife crisis.

Chapter 4

The world is changing and being in it is just making it even worst. I wish I just could make the world do what I want. Today I decided that I will tell my parents and boyfriend that I am a mermaid. "Hey mom" I said. "What is it" mom replied, I responded by saying "I'm a mermaid look at my tail". My mom rushed in the bathroom and saw my tail and then my dad came. They both were so scared and told me I should tell Chris. I called Chris while I was still in the bathtub and asked him to come over ASAP. After 10 minutes Chris arrived and ran to my bathroom he saw my tail and asked if this was a joke or something. I told him to look closely and do you think I would lie about such thing. My parents and Chris all passed out when they awoke I got out the bathtub. "What are you doing in my house I don't even know you" said my mom. Wait hold on I don't know what is going on we were just talking. I spoke up and replied "it's me your daughter Tay Tay, mom you must know me, dad, Chris, mom I love you guys please remember".

“how do you know my name"

“Chris you don't remember".

I started to cry, I felt my heart stop beating and I almost passed out. I fell to the ground and started to hyperventilate. My mom brought me over to the couch and fanned me. "Sweetie do you know where your real parents are" my dad asked. How could they not remember me? I got up and looked to see if my room is still there but it just had my stuff packed. "Who is this" I asked. "Oh that's our daughter she died a year ago" replied mom. I looked at the picture that's me how could they not remember me. Suddenly there was a knock on the door. When I saw my parents open it I saw that lady I forgot her name. But then I remembered I screamed out of nowhere

"LAYLA LAYLA ITS ME TAYLOR I JUST TOLD THEM THE SECRET AND NOW THEY DONT REMEMBER ME". Layla looked up and replied "oh my baby Taylor I missed you sweetie stop running away". What I don't even know where she lives. This is my family, why is everyone acting so weird? Why can't they remember me? I ran over and grabbed the frame of me. I help it up to my face. "Look this is me I am not dead I am your daughter and I have always been..." I stopped when I heard someone crying. I looked around and saw my mom crying. "May you get out our house are daughter is dead we put her in the ground now if you don't mind GET OUT OUR HOUSE" said my dad. I looked at him and just left. I can't believe he could be so cruel. How is this?

Chapter 5

I walked out the house while crying, "Are you crazy Taylor, Mermaid World could be destroyed why now, all your being is just selfish"!! Said Layla. "Well you never

had a family so, you don't know what it feels like to lose someone". I replied.
"Actually I used have one but, since you want to be mean fine BYE!!"
I walked around trying to figure out what to do. I just thought about a way for them to remember me. MY Book!! Maybe if I find it, I can find a way to get my identity back. I just don't know where all my things are but, I made a plan on what to do. When it hits midnight, I will sneak in the house go through the boxes and see if it's there hopefully it is.
When it hit midnight I snuck in the window and went up the steps. I saw my room I went in there and searched the boxes but, no book. So, I decided to look inside the drawers but, nothing how could this be. That's when I decided to check under a piece of wood that hasn't been fixed and it was there. I grabbed it and ran out the house. When I got to a nice seating area, I sat down and tried to find how to get your identity back. The closest thing I found is how to get out of deep situations. I just had to call on Layla so, I did. Layla didn't come how could she do this to me. She should know what I am going through and she should support me. I have no one now and I am just lost. That's when I decided to talk to Chris.
"I am here what do you want" said Layla. She showed up. Really? That's a surprise.
"You showed up"
"Yea is that a surprise"
"Kind of"
"Anyway what do you want?"

“My identity back”
She looked at me crazy for a long time and didn’t say anything. “Umm it’s not that easy”. Well I knew that, at 1 minute I am someone different the other I am me. It is not science.

Chapter 6

All I want is my life back why can't I just have one good thing happen to me.
"I love my parents I really do"

"Well you should have thought about it"

"I thought I was just going to lose my legs, I was up for that not this"

"You know I can't give their memories back you have to go to the mermaid’s authorities yourself"

"How do I get there?"

"Hold on, here is my wand bee do beep bop do"

Where am I? I looked up and I saw the sign "Mermaid authorities". I opened the door and there were so many mermaids. I saw the room that said "Questions" so I went

in there. *Why am I here again, oh yea I need help, I thought.*
"Um Hi, I am Taylor..."

"Yea yea we know who you are Taylor, you want your identity back"

"Well can I"

"It's not that simple you know. We need to see if you're worthy enough"

"I am I promise"

"There is only one way to prove it"

"How tell me please!!!!!!"

"You have 24 hours to bring the emerald necklace back to us"

"Ok where is it"

"That is part of the quest"

Chapter 7

The first place I looked at was "The diamond tower". There were 100 stairs so I knew I had to look fast.

"You didn't think I would let you search alone"

"Thanks' Layla, but don't you have better things to do"

"No I rather help my daughter lol"

"Ok well let's start looking"

When we got to the 100th floor there was nothing. I looked at my watch and it's already been 5 hours. I need to think harder.
"Taylor, what about your house"

"Ok, but how exactly am I supposed to get in their without being kicked out"

"Well, haven't you heard of distractions?"

We talked about the plan for 5 minutes and so we went. I climbed up the window into my room while Layla distracted them. I searched the boxes and under the bed. I couldn't find it I knew I searched well. Then it came to me the picture frame. I opened the frame of me at the beach and their I saw a map leading me to the necklace. I climbed out the window and whistled. A few moments later Layla came out.
"Well did you get it"

"No, but I got a map leading to it"

"Hand it to me"

I handed her the map. She stood there for a while looking at flipping it over and over.
"How do you know that it is for the emerald necklace?"
"........ It was behind my picture frame of me at the beach and you know mermaids..... Water"

"Ok whatever we have to go now.

We drove in the direction the map told us but slowly the map started to fade. How exactly am I supposed to get a quest that is impossible? I drove faster to get to the destination before the map could fade.

"Slow your role Taylor I might be a mermaid but, I can still die"

"Sorry it's the map it is starting to fade"

"Oh well speed up.... but first let me tighten my seat belt"

I sped up the car and the map just started to fade faster. Luckily, I arrived at the destination. I looked around and I was at the beach. I looked at the map and everything was gone everything. *The ocean maybe it's underneath it.* I jumped in the ocean and started looking. *Oh great I forgot I was a mermaid I do not need air right now*. I got deeper and deeper and all I saw were a bunch of mermaids. The necklace there it is.

"Taylor STOP"

"Why, there is the necklace"

"I know I see but, some mermaids are dangerous and their one of them"
"I am sure we can make reasoning"

I swam lower to where the mermaid with the necklace was. I asked "Can I have your necklace it is just so lovely"? "GUARDS" Yelled all of the mermaids. They started shooting arrows at me. I swam to the top of the ocean and got rescue.
"Well what did I tell you?"

"Whatever how am I supposed to get the necklace?"

"It's all in the mission"

"Can everyone stop saying it's in the mission and give me an actual clue"

I sat down on the sand and tried think of a good plan. Nothing came to mind. I just feel helpless and I want help.

"Oh yea I can read your mind"

"Oh, then try reading this"

I hate this stupid mission. I hate being a mermaid. I WANT MY LIFE BACK!! I don't like my mermaid self, I like my human self. I don't want to be stuck like this got it if I could change it.

"Well I didn't put you like this you know what you're a .... a brat"

"Maybe I am but, I just want to have my life back"

"I KNOW YOU KEEP SAYING THAT"

"I'm going back under"

"Be safe"

I swam in the water again and the guards were still there they didn't move. I hid behind the wall and the mermaid was again. She had worry on her face and she had her hand wrapped around the necklace, like she knew I was coming for it. I walked in slowly when she was all alone. "Please hear me out, as you can see I am a mermaid too. I want my family to have their memory back that I am their child"

"You don't get it, I am the necklace by the way I'm Fiara"

"But, that can't be what is that your neck"

"A necklace but its diamond not emerald"

“Oh”

How exactly and I supposed to capture I can’t that is plain evil.

Chapter 8

"So you’re the emerald necklace"

"Yes"

"But.......how"

"Well... your here from the Mermaid counsel right"

"No I was just trying to find the emerald necklace everyone is looking for by the way, can you come with me will quick"

"Ok"

She must be an air head if she will follow. I mean she knows I am about to capture her. I really don't care as long as my parents get their memory back. When I got to the top of the water I saw Layla just sitting there.

"Layla how come you didn't get in the water?"

"I haven't told you this but I haven't swam in a while"

I just looked at her and told her that Fiana was the emerald necklace. After, I told her she took Fiana and started flying like..... Like a... She's a vampire. How am I supposed to get Fiana back? I just don't like this. I trusted Fiana I thought we were great friends. I trusted her.
I just can't believe Fiana's gone and she was taking by my so call "Friend and mermaid". I actually thought things were going good but, again I should have known something bad was going to happen. I started walking and thinking how to get to the Mermaid Counsel. I started to believe and I got there. So, all that time believing is my magic power. I opened up the counsel door and walked in the same people from last were here again.
"Hear me out, Layla isn't a mermaid I thought she was I got Fiana but then Layla took her. I swear I will get her I just need more time"

"Well you better start now because you only have 6 hours left"

"What I ju....."

Before I could finish I was back on land. I tried to think and think of a way to find them. Nothing came to mind. The book it just appeared in my hand. I searched through it and I couldn't find anything.

Chapter 9

"I GOT IT SENSE"

I looked up and everyone was staring at me. But, I didn't care because I was just happy I found a way to find them. My mermaid senses. When I was sensing for them I guess I found other mermaids. I walked up a lot of hills I was so tired.

"Ha Fiana after all these years trying to find you aka the "emerald necklace" my "client" found you" said Layla.

"Get me out of here" said Fiana.

"Your powers are everything so, just stay still and you will be OK"

"What exactly are you trying to do"

"I will just inject this needle into your heart and place the other end into this ball"

"You won't get away with this and what exactly do you want my powers for. You're a vampire and vampires can't use mermaid powers"

"Exactly, mermaids think they're the best. Vampires will be the best. I am so sick of being unknown and no one talking about but, just finally I have the opportunity, now stop moving"

Layla got the needle out and stuck it into Fiana's heart. She didn't have enough time because I arrived. When I

tried to step in I passed out I guess it was an Anti - Mermaid fence. When I woke up I only had two hours left. I got up and tried to think of a way to get through it. I didn't want to go back to council because I bugged them way too much.
"Pssst...... Fiana how do I get passed here" I said.

"I can try hitting the off button but, it will take a while"
"Ok"

While Fiana was trying to hit the button I was looking out for Taylor. It was a scary process because I didn't know who we were messing with. I wasn't trying to get killed.

"Stop she's coming" I whispered.

I guess Fiana didn't hear me because she kept trying to get to it. I got back on the ground like I was before. I closed my eyes and tried to listen very closely. I couldn't hear much but, I heard on word that came from Layla I'm not sure. The word was "magic". Like she wanted magic. But, why did she want magic, what's so great about magic? With my eyes closed I started to think about believing. I started to believe I could get past the fence. When I opened my eyes I was inside the fence. Layla didn't see me so, I turned the Anti-Mermaid fence off for when I escape this crazy place on top of a roof. Who does that?

"Taylor, I don't want to hurt you so just leave?

"I am not leaving you are a monster, Layla a true one"

"Taylor, listen to her I will be fine" said Fiana.

"I am not leaving Layla, let Fiana go now" I said.

Before I could do anything I saw Layla running to me with a bat. I dodged quickly and made a quick move. I untied Fiana and started running. I believed that we were back in Fiana's home and we were.

"Thanks, but why didn't you take me to the counsel"

"You don't deserve too. I see you have a normal life. I was being selfish earlier and I need to live with being a mermaid"

"Well thanks, you can hang out you know"

"Ok, why do people want you?"

"Sit down and I will tell you"

Ok I sat down on her pretty flower couch of course under water and I listened to the story.

Chapter 10

"My mother and father weren't mermaids when they got married. They both loved to go swimming. This ocean was their favorite. When my mom got pregnant with me, she didn't go swimming for a while until 27 weeks. When she did go swimming it was in this ocean. I guess there was a mermaid in the ocean and it bit my mom. My dad rushed her to the hospital but, while they were going they got sent to the Mermaid counsel. They told them that my mom was a mermaid and they made my dad one too. They sent my mom to the mermaid hospital and made her give birth to protect the baby. I came out glowing and an emerald stuck to my chest and so, I got the nickname "Emerald Necklace. I wasn't even premature so, my mom wanted to name me Miracle but, my dad wanted Fiana because Fin as in tale is in it. I grew up very fast and I never age."

"Wow, I never heard a story like that before"

"Yeah but, they just want to take my powers and looks"

"Well you are a pretty mermaid"

"Yeah I just wish I had the perfect guy and not something that came from my powers"

"I know what you mean"

"Do you have a special someone?"

"Actually yes, but he doesn't remember me because I told him I was a mermaid"

"Oh true, that's why I live in the ocean because no one will find out about my identity by the way, your tell is very beautiful"

"Well I better get going thanks anyway"

"No problem"

I swam up and rested on the sand. I thought about how wonderful her story was. A bright was all around and I was back with the mermaid counsel.

"I guess my time is up"

"Yes and you don't have the emerald necklace"

"Will my family get their memories back"

"NO! You don't have the emerald necklace get out of here"

I didn't leave mermaid land. I was still here just in a house that had my name on it. I walked out the house and tried to believe to get back on Earth but, it didn't work. I was stuck here. I need to find a way out of here. I started walking around asking people how to leave here. I got nothing except for you can't. I did find one person that said I am in sometime of prison because I didn't get what the counsel wanted.

I tried to get more information but, I decided to go rest. I had a pretty long day. I went looking around my house I guess to find my bed. "Aha there it is" I found it on the 2nd floor I guess this house has three because that's all I've seen. I laid down and thought of great things. I started to think of when my tucked me in at night and told me how much she loved me. I miss those days. While thinking this my eyes slowly shut and I went to sleep.

Chapter 11

I got out of bed and looked out the window. I saw a lot of mermaids walking around. I turned to look at the clock it was 10:30 am. I went downstairs and looked in the refrigerator to see if there was any food. "Cool my favorite foods, just no breakfast ugh" I said out loud like some complete weirdo. I grabbed the milk and looked around for the dining table. I walked around for a while then I found it. I sat down while I drank. When I was done I got back up and left "my" house.

"Where am I" I asked some girl.

"Were in Mermaid Lock up, it's when you don't do what the Mermaid Counsel tells you to do" said the girl.

"Oh, by the way my name is Taylor what is your name"

"My name is Jazzy, how about you come to my house and we can talk"

"Ok"

I walked to Jazzy's house. When we got there she told me that we can't talk in public because some of these people you can't trust them. We started to walk to her house when we arrived her house was so beautiful it was a pretty pink and had chandeliers everywhere. Her chairs were beautiful of course, pink but it was soft and clean.

"Wow I really need to decorate "my house" I said

"It took me a while to decorate anyway sit down so we can talk"

I sat down on the couch and waited for Jazzy to come back with some tea.

"Ok, sorry we had to talk privately but we could get killed if we talk out in public"

"That's fine but, where is Mermaid Lock up exactly" I asked taking a sip of tea.

"It's in the sky I guess no one has left here. If they did they were probably killed when they found out"

"That's crazy I have to get back to my family they already forgot about me. I helped the counsel they should be praising me right now and I should be with my family"

"I mean you had to do something wrong if you're here"

"Oh, I did get her but didn't bring her to them anyways, I guess I am going to be here for a while do you want to help me decorate my house tomorrow"

"Sure no problem bye"

I got up from the couch and put my pink tea cup that said "I heart Mermaids" on the table and walked to the door with Jazzy. She opened the door and said bye I replied and walked back home until I got lost. Eventually, I made it back. I went in and got some dinner. I had Fried chicken, mashed potatoes and Kool-Aid. When I was done I went upstairs and tried to find my dresser. AHA there it is. It was right in front of my bed. How did I not see it? I found some cute pink pajamas with a smiley face on the shirt. I took a shower then put my pajamas on.

Just when I was about to get in my bed I heard a knock on the door. "OPEN UP NOW" someone yelled. I ran downstairs and opened the door. Some guy put a bag over my head and put me in a truck. When I woke up I was in a black room with little lights sitting in a chair with my hands tied..

"I've seen you have woken up" said some guy.

"Huh where am I what are you going to do" I replied

"Oh right I am Jordan you went too far and you know too much"

"What do you mean, WHAT ARE YOU GOING TO DO!!!!?"

"You're not going to be telling anybody anything you're going on a little trip"

Jordan grabbed my arm and pulled me off the chair he still didn't untie me. We were walking through a long hallway with 4 men. I must be somewhere far from Mermaid Lock Up. I was scared from my family not remembering me to some random guys taking me somewhere I don't even know and claim I'm going on a trip. I saw a door and I knew this was the time to make a run for it. I kicked Jordan in the leg and ran for the door. Out there was nothing for me to walk on just midair and land on the ground I had to jump.

“WAIT! You don’t want to do that you don’t know what’s down there”

“Right and I don’t even know what you guys are going to do to me so I think I will take my chances”

“Taylor I love you so much don’t do this”

“How do you know my name and how can you love me, I don’t know you”

“Come back here and I will tell you”

I didn’t know what to think. He said he loved me and I don’t even know him. I looked at the ground outside I think and I looked back at Jordan. I kept debating what I should I do but, I decided. I closed the door and told Jordan to explain.

“I’m your older brother everything that’s happening to you happened to me”

“But, why did you do all of this”

“I was demanded too by the council”

“Oh, but how can you love me when you don’t know me?”

“That’s because I tuck you in at night and I read to you and…. I’m like your guardian angel”

“You don’t read to me and tuck me in”

“Yes I do it’s just you can’t hear or feel me so, you don’t know”

I was confused I didn’t know what to believe.

www.ingramcontent.com/pod-product-compliance
Ingram Content Group UK Ltd.
Pitfield, Milton Keynes, MK11 3LW, UK
UKHW020229250726
13967UKWH00001B/260

9 781329 078017